Dudley the Dinosaur

Short Stories, Games, Jokes, and More!

Uncle Amon

Published by Hey Sup Bye Publishing

ISBN-13: 978-1534758186
ISBN-10: 1534758186

TABLE OF CONTENTS

Enter Dudley

Once upon a time, a few hundred million years ago, the world was a very different place. There were not seven continents on earth, as there are now, there was only one: a huge, supercontinent that we call Pangaea.

And there were no people wandering around at all. Instead, the earth was dominated by towering reptiles called dinosaurs, a word which means "terrible lizards," though some were perfectly pleasant.

There were a great many kinds of dinosaurs and, just like with people, some of them were very kind and some of them were not.

One of the nicest of these dinos was named Dudley. He was a little small for his age, he was pinkish purple, and he loved to run and growl. He was really great at growling.

More than anything, Dudley wanted to make friends. But he had a problem. Dudley was a Tyrannosaurus Rex, and T. Rexes were the most feared creatures in the entire world!

The words Tyrannosaurus Rex mean "tyrant lizard" which is not a name that really makes you want to hang out with a fellow. T. Rexes had twelve-inch long, razor sharp teeth and powerful legs that could propel them toward their prey at, some people say, as much as forty-five miles per hour!

T. Rexes were, in one word: reallysupercrazyscary!

Dudley would never harm a fly, but everyone was terrified of him anyway just because of what he was. He would walk up to other dinosaurs on the playground and politely say, "Hello! My name is Dudley. How are you today?"

And the other kids would always respond the same way. They would scream at the top of their lungs and then run away as fast as their little dino feet could carry them.

It made Dudley sad. He had a lot of love to share and he knew he could be a really good friend if someone would just give him a chance. He wouldn't eat his pals or anything, even if he missed lunch or something!

But one day, as Dudley was walking home from school, he came across several of his classmates in a clearing. A pterodactyl named Terry, a triceratops named Biscuit, and a stegosaurus named Enrique. They were all three being bullied by a nasty velociraptor named Franklin. Velociraptors were all dangerous. They were fast and strong, they had talons like a reapers scythe and teeth like razor wire strung through a jaw like a steel trap! They were smaller than you probably think, about the size of a big chicken, but they were mean-spirited.

And Franklin was much older than the other dinos. He was a high school lizard while the others were all still in the first grade.

Dudley was scared, heck, he was terrified, but he knew he had to help. And he had been practicing his very excellent roar!

So Dudley stepped out of the jungle, stood right between his classmates and Franklin, stood tall, and roar his biggest, best roar ever!

Franklin didn't wait for a second roar! He turned straight around and sprinted into the jungle, away from the mighty T. Rex!

Dudley turned back to his classmates with a smile, feeling good that he had been able to help even though he was scared.

But Terry, Biscuit, and Enrique just screamed even louder than before!

"Great!" Terry said. "We were going to be eaten by a raptor, and instead we get eaten by a T. Rex!"

"No!" Dudley said, but then he was interrupted by Biscuit.

"I don't know what you're complaining about, Terry! You can just fly away."

"Oh yeah!" Terry said. And then he just flew away.

"Dang it, Biscuit!" Enrique said. "It was three against one! We might have had a chance!"

"Guys!" Dudley said. "It's not any against any! I'm not going to eat you! I'm nice and also I just filled up on crackers and fruit snacks!"

"So why did you roar at us like that?" Enrique asked.

"I was scaring away the raptor!" Dudley answered.

"So…you were helping us?" said Biscuit. "Kind of like…like a friend?"

"Not kind of like, EXACTLY like a friend!" Dudley said. He then added, "I mean, I think so. I don't know. I've never had a friend before."

"Well," Enrique said, "now you have two."

"Three!" Terry said, floating gently to the ground.

"I'm still pretty mad at you!" Biscuit said to Terry.

Terry opened the mighty talons on one of his feet revealing a treat. "I brought pie!" he said.

"Then you are forgiven," Biscuit offered.

And so the four friends gladly ate pie together, none quite realizing that a lifelong bond had been formed that day, but very happy all the same.

Fly Away Home

Dudley the dinosaur had finally made his first friends and he was very excited about that. For all of his life the other lizards had all been too scared to get to know him. They thought that just because he was a Tyrannosaurus Rex, Dudley would automatically want to eat them, so they never even gave him a chance. They never got close enough to Dudley to discover that he was much fonder of chowing down on peanut butter and jelly sandwiches than his classmates.

But after Dudley helped a few other dinos out of a tough spot they all became very close. They went almost everywhere and did nearly everything together.

Swimming in the pond, boulder bowling, you name it and Dudley, Frank, Enrique and Biscuit probably did it as one.

It was the happiest time of Dudley's young life and he was careful to savor each moment with his friends and to be grateful for them all.

But there were some places Dudley just couldn't go. Frank was a pterodactyl you see, and pterodactyls are a kind of dinosaur that could fly.

Frank could soar through the air with the greatest of ease! He could travel miles and miles without breaking a sweat! And Dudley was a little jealous of this. He wanted to fly, too!

So Dudley started simple. First he just jumped up and down as high as he could, flapping his tiny, ridiculous T. Rex arms to take flight. To the surprise of absolutely no one, that didn't work.

"My arms are small and basically just silly," Dudley said to no one in particular. "But my tail is long and mighty! The answer is in my tail!"

So Dudley crouched low to the ground, held his tail high above him and spun it just as quickly as he could! His tail whooshed as it ripped through the air, but he did not take flight.

"This is discouraging," Dudley said, still talking to really no one at all. "The problem is that I do not have wings! I should get some of those!"

So Dudley first made a frame out of twigs, which he held together with vines. He lashed together several dozen banana peels in between the twigs to fill out the wings.

He climbed high atop a tall volcano, strapped the wings on his back and said, "Well, here goes nothing!"

He leapt from the mountain and almost immediately his wings broke apart and he sank like a stone! As he fell he said, "I suppose there's a reason wings are not made of bananas and sticks."

He then said, "I suppose, also, that this is the end for me. I had a good run."

The ground rose up to meet him. It got closer and closer and poor Dudley braced for impact. And then the strangest thing happened: he didn't die. And the ground started to get farther and farther away!

"I'm flying!" Dudley shouted!

"Of course you're not flying, silly. I am," Frank said.

Dudley looked up to find that Frank had caught him and was now carrying him to safety.

Frank asked his friend, "Are you trying to get yourself killed, buddy?"

"No," Dudley said. "I just wanted to be more like you."

"Well," Frank answered, "I think you'd be much better of just being yourself. Who you are is great! You can't fly, no. But I can't scare off dangerous villains! We're all special in our own way."

Dudley thought on that for a while before saying, "You're right. I have to be the best ME I can be, not the best you! Now that that's settled let's get pie!"

Frank laughed and said, "I guess we're all the same in at least one way: everyone loves pie."

Faster Than A Speeding Turtle! But Just Barely

Enrique was an adorable stegosaurus. A few hundred million years in the future he would become the official state dinosaur of Colorado, but at the time that this story takes place he was just a kid with a dream.

If there's one thing everyone knows about a stegosaurus it's that they have large plates rising out of their backs, and long, sharp spikes on their tails.

What many people don't know is that those famous plates actually grew out of their skin, rather than being attached to their bones. That fact has literally nothing to do with this story, it's just neat.

Another thing many people don't know is that, because of their short, squat legs, a stegosaurus had a top speed of around five miles per hour. I guess when you have super sharp, two-foot long spikes on your powerful tail you don't need to run from very many things, but in Enrique's case his lack of speed was an issue because he really wanted to make it onto his school's track team.

One of Enrique's very best friends was a Tyrannosaurus Rex named Dudley. And T. Rexes had a maximum speed of up to forty-five miles an hour! So Enrique asked if Dudley could help make him fast.

"I want to be a champion sprinter!" Enrique said.

"Right," Dudley said. "Well, I think the biggest problem you're going to face is the fact that you're a stegosaurus. So can you be something else? Like a cat?"

"I don't think I can, no," Enrique answered.

"Fair enough," Dudley said. "I'm just thinking out loud. Just spitballing. There are no such things as bad ideas."

"I think maybe there are," Enrique said. "I think that was one of them."

Dudley thought on the situation for a moment and said, "Well, there's only one substitute for natural talent and that's hard work."

Enrique's eyes perked up. "Let's do it!"

So for the next ten weeks Enrique and Dudley woke up at the crack of dawn and ran until sunset. They ran up mountains and through valleys and streams. When Enrique was so tired he thought he would never be able to take another step, Dudley would gently gnaw on his tail to motivate him! And then he would run and run some more.

When the day came to try out for the track team, with Dudley cheering him on, Enrique ran the 100-meter dash at just over six miles an hour! That made him the fastest stegosaurus who ever lived! And it was still WAY too slow to make it on the team as a sprinter.

"I guess sometimes you can try your best and still not win," Enrique said, a little sad but also very proud of how hard he had worked.

And just as Enrique was about to head back home, the coach of the team, a very nice hypacrosaurus named Lilly trotted over to him and said, "I've been watching you run for the last few weeks. By the end of your training you could run all day without stopping. I don't think you'll ever be a sprinter, but I can't think of any other dinosaur I'd rather have run the two-mile event for me. What do you say?"

"I say yes!" Enrique yelled, unable to contain his joy!

Slow and steady is how he ran, and won, every race that year.

Sometimes we don't even realize all that we have accomplished, but hard work always pays off one way or another.

Dino-Dentistry

Biscuit was an odd sort of fellow. He was a triceratops, which is a word that means "three horned face" but, like all triceratops, he really only had two horns and that kind of freaked him out a little.

He felt like since his very face was misunderstood, no one could ever really come to know him honestly. To know whom he really, truly was.

Little did he know that, for various reasons, most dinosaurs, and most people, feel the exact same way from time to time.

The two proper horns that all triceratops have are easy to see. They are long (up to three feet long!) and sharp. The confusion comes in the third "horn" on their snout, which was not really a horn at all. It was more of a bump made of soft proteins, very much like what a human's fingernails are made of. You could call it a horn, most people did, but did that make it true? Would a kitten become a puppy if you just called it that long enough? Questions like these kept him up at night. He was very much afraid that if he ever found an answer he would somehow grow up to be a politician.

Perhaps the oddest thing about Biscuit, though, (even more odd than being named Biscuit) was that we was obsessed with oral hygiene.

"Your teeth are the best friends you've got. You take care of them and they will take care of you." That was his motto.

And a good motto it is! Your teeth are incredibly important and need to be taken care of extremely well every single day with regular combinations of brushing, flossing, and mouthwash.

But at some point Biscuit started taking care of his teeth to the point that it got dangerous.

First he stopped eating sweets, which was a good idea. Then he stopped eating all together, which was a very bad idea.

When his friends and family tried to convince him to nourish himself with food, he would only say, "If I never eat, my teeth will never stain, I'll never get a cavity and they will always be perfect."

Everyone was very worried about him. So his newest friend Dudley, a young T. Rex went to see him.

"Your teeth are a gift," Dudley said. "No one appreciates their teeth more than a T. Rex. We use them all the time to hunt and rip up…um…" it was at that point that Dudley realized he was surrounded by dinosaurs that, traditionally, are eaten by T. Rexes, so he said, "pie! We use them to hunt pie. But they're a gift like golf clubs or a ratchet set. You take care of them so you can always use them. They are tools meant to be used!"

"I think you're right," Biscuit agreed. "I want to be passionate about taking care of my teeth. Passion is good, but obsession is not. And I'm SUPER hungry."

Everyone smiled and sighed in relief. Their friend was going to be okay. They knew that for sure when next Biscuit spoke saying, "So…who's got the pie?"

The answer was everyone. Everyone had brought pies of all kinds. They ate the treats all-night and laughed and talked and all was well in the world.

Bad Decisions

Not to be unkind, but in all honesty dinosaurs were not really the brightest creatures to ever walk the earth. The smartest dino that ever lived so far as we know (troodon) had at his command intelligence that would easily be outpaced by that of a one-day-old cat.

But, while troodon was the brightest, the very dumbest may have very well been a young Apatosaurus named Bruno.

One day, when he was full grown, Bruno would measure seventy-five feet from nose to tail and tip the scales at an incredible forty tons! Equal to a dozen elephants or more!

One day the very earth beneath his feet would tremble as he walked, but for the moment he was just a kid in the third grade that had his head stuck in a beehive.

That's where he was when Dudley, a young T. Rex walked by.

"Ow." Slurp! "Ow." Slurp. Came the repeated sounds from inside the hive.

"Um...are you okay in there?" Dudley asked, pretty sure he knew the answer already.

"Well," Bruno answered, "yes and no. Yes because I am eating delicious honey, which was my goal, and no because OUCH, I am getting stung by bees A LOT!"

"I see," Dudley said. "Have you considered removing your head from the beehive?"

"It hadn't occurred to me," Bruno confessed. "It's worth a try!" But as the young Apatosaurus tried to retreat he found his head, which had managed to fit quite well on the way in, was now having great difficulty getting out. Worse than that, his attempts to leave agitated the bees even further and now they were stinging him more than ever! "Owowowowowow!"

"I think I have the answer!" Dudley proclaimed proudly. He had been reading books about the great dino detective Sherlockosaurus Holmes, who did himself keep bees. Sherlockosaurus always blew smoke into his beehives in order to calm the bees before he harvested their honey. So Dudley found two flint stones nearby, gathered up some dry leaves and cracked the stones together. A spark shot off the rocks, landed on the leaves and they caught fire with a whoosh!

The smoke from the flames rose fast and black. It found its way inside the hive and almost immediately the bees all took a nap!

"It worked!" Bruno yelled.

"Shush." Dudley scolded. "You don't want to wake them again." Dudley then broke open some nearby aloe plants and spread their lotion around Bruno's head as far as he could reach. Next he grabbed Bruno's tail in his mighty jaws and gave him a great yank!

Bruno's head popped free of the hive and he was so happy to be out that he gave Dudley a big dino hug!

The two lizards headed out of the jungle and back toward town.

"How can I ever thank you?" Bruno asked.

"Just be more careful!" Dudley said. "Sometimes the things we want are bad for us. So we have to be smart about what we do."

"That makes sense," Bruno said. But the words were oddly muffled.

Dudley looked back to find Bruno's head was stuck inside another beehive. "What?" Dudley asked in disbelief.

"Can I start being smarter tomorrow?" Bruno said. "I really like honey."

Dudley laughed, shook his head, and started looking around for more flint rocks and dried leaves.

Funny Dinosaur Jokes

Q: What type of tools did cave men use?

A: A dino-saw!

Q: What's the scariest dinosaur?

A: A terror-dactyl!

Q: What makes more noise than a dinosaur?

A: A group of dinosaurs!

Q: What do you call a dinosaur with a large vocabulary?

A: A thesaurus!

Q: What did you call a dinosaur that keeps you awake at night?

A: Bronto-snore-us!

Q: Which dinosaur can jump higher than a house?

A: All of them. Houses don't jump!

Q: Why did the dinosaurs eat raw food?

A: They did not know how to cook!

Q: Why did the dinosaur cross the road?

A: Because the chicken wasn't invented yet!

Q: What do you say to a twenty-ton dinosaur with headphones on?

A: Anything you want. He can't hear you!

Q: Why didn't the T-Rex skeleton attack the museum visitors?

A: Because he had no guts!

Q: What do you get when you put TNT and a dinosaur together?

A: Dino-mite!

Q: What do you call a blind dinosaur?

A: Do-ya-think-he-saurus!

Q: What was the most flexible dinosaur?

A: Tyrannosaurus Flex!

Q: Why did the Apatosaurus devour the factory?

A: Because she was a plant eater!

Q: What are prehistoric monsters called when they sleep?

A: A dinosnore!

Q: What dinosaur would you find in a rodeo?

A: Bronco-saurus!

Games and Puzzles

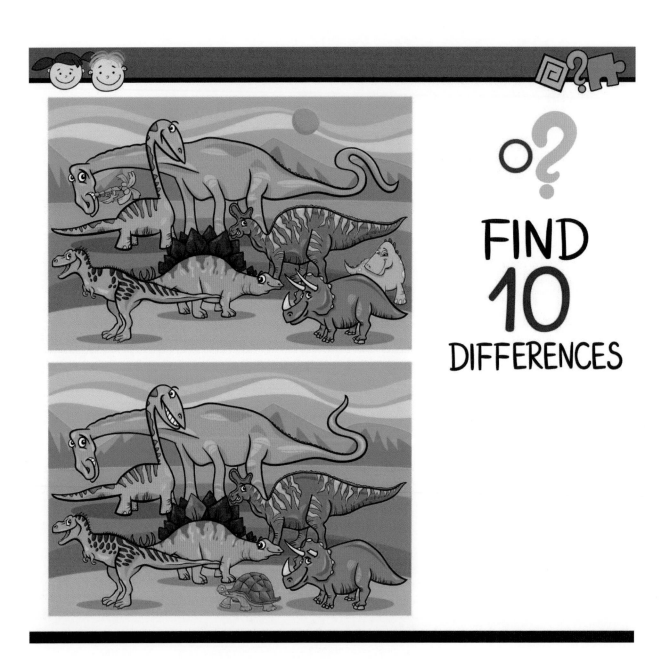

FIND 10 DIFFERENCES

How Many Dinosaurs?

Maze #1

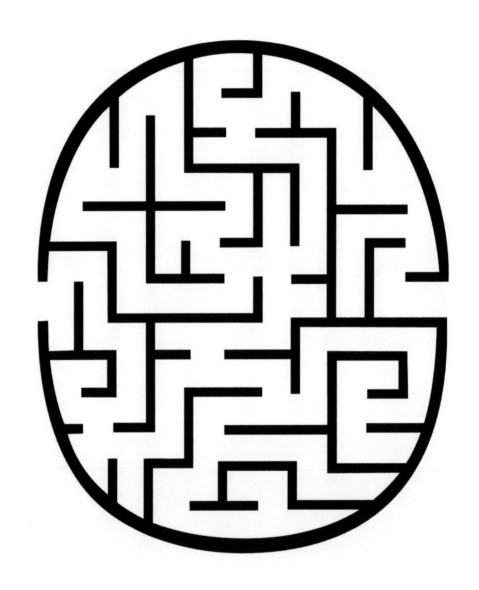

Maze #2

Maze #3

Maze #4

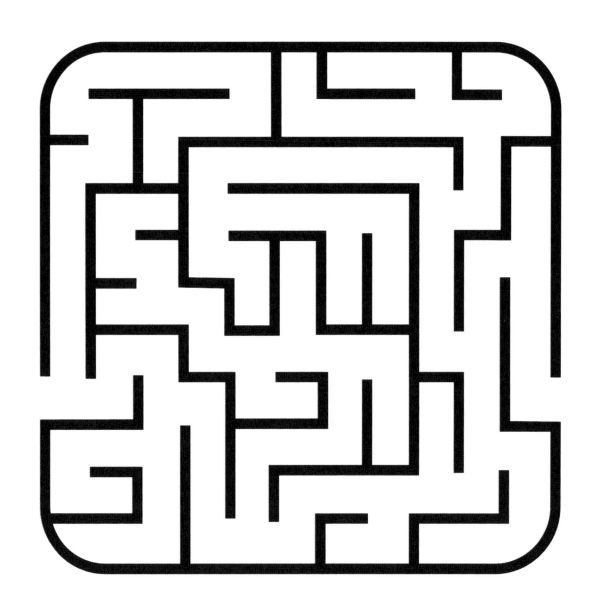

Game and Puzzle Solutions

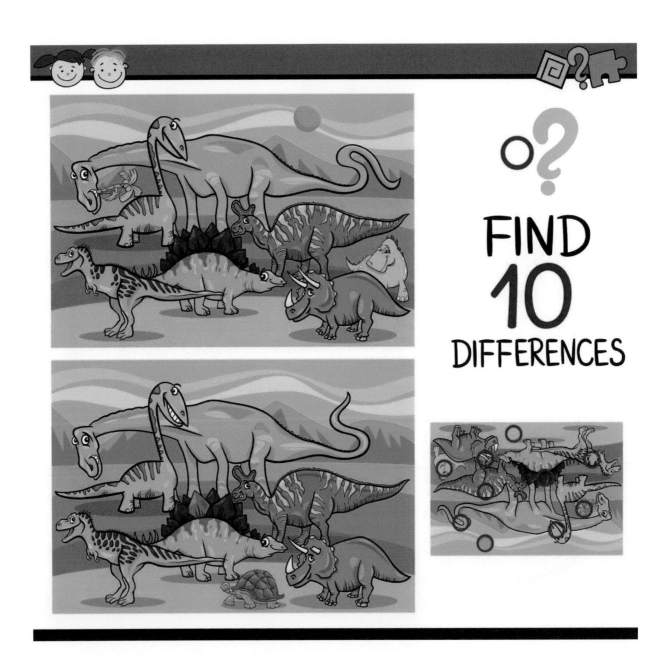

FIND
10
DIFFERENCES

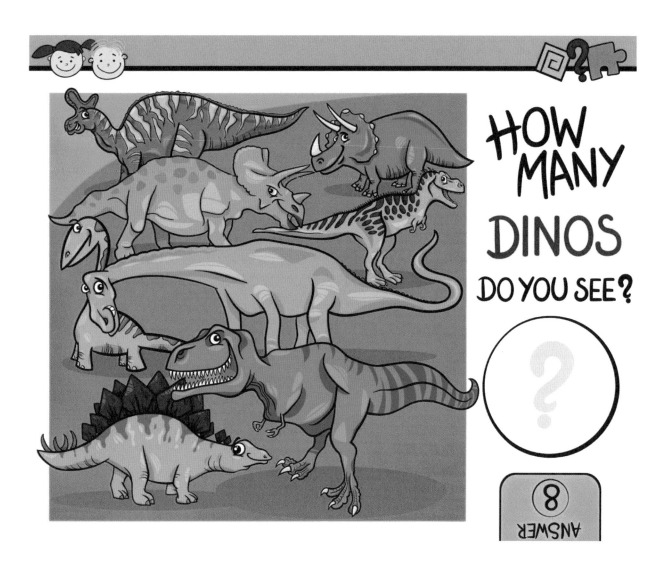

HOW MANY DINOS DO YOU SEE?

?

ANSWER ⑧

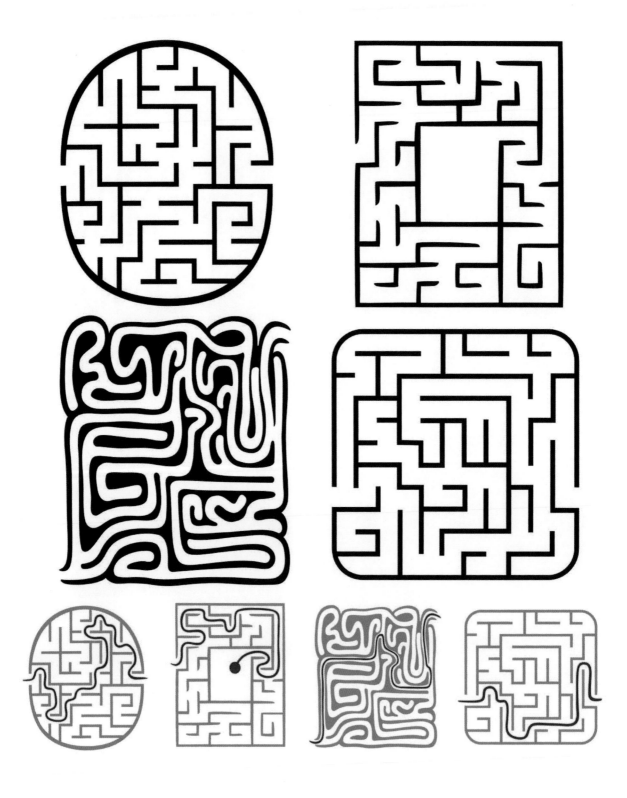

ABOUT THE AUTHOR

Uncle Amon began his career with a vision. It was to influence and create a positive change in the world through children's books by sharing fun and inspiring stories. Whether it is an important lesson or just creating laughs, Uncle Amon provides insightful stories that are sure to bring a smile to your face! His unique style and creativity stand out from other children's book authors, because he uses real life experiences to tell a tale of imagination and adventure.

"I always shoot for the moon. And if I miss? I'll land in the stars."
-Uncle Amon

Printed in Great Britain
by Amazon